Odysseus
and the
Wooden Horse

First published in 2008 by
Franklin Watts
338 Euston Road
London
NW1 3BH

Franklin Watts Australia
Level 17/207 Kent Street
Sydney
NSW 2000

A CIP catalogue record for this book is available
from the British Library.

ISBN 978 0 7496 7994 1 (hbk)
ISBN 978 0 7496 8002 2 (pbk)

Series Editor: Melanie Palmer
Series Advisor: Dr Barrie Wade
Series Designer: Peter Scoulding

Printed in China

Franklin Watts is a division of
Hachette Children's Books,
an Hachette Livre UK company
www.hachettelivre.co.uk

Odysseus
and the
Wooden Horse

by Damian Harvey and Martin Remphry

FRANKLIN WATTS

LONDON•SYDNEY

Long ago, the Trojans and the
Greeks were at war. The Trojan
king sent his sons, Hector and
Paris, to Greece to make peace.

But in Greece, Paris fell in love with the Greek king's beautiful wife, Helen. He took her back to Troy.

The king of Greece was furious. He gathered his armies, led by mighty Odysseus. They sailed to Troy to bring Helen back.

Outside the walls of Troy there was a great battle. Each side sent their best fighters. Odysseus chose the Greek heroes, Ajax and Achilles.

The Trojans chose their princes,
Hector and Paris. The others
hid behind the huge city walls.

First Ajax swung his huge hammer at Hector, but he missed. Hector knocked Ajax down.

Then Hector was hit by the spear of Achilles, the greatest Greek warrior of all.

Next Paris took out his arrow and shot Achilles in the heel. The great Achilles fell down dead.

Odysseus was shocked to see his
best soldier killed. "We must get
into the city of Troy," he said.

13

But the Greeks could not break into the city. The walls were too high and the gates were too strong.

Then clever Odysseus had an idea.
"Build me a great wooden horse,"
he ordered. "Make it big enough
for me and my men to fit inside."

For many days and nights the Greeks worked hard to build a huge wooden horse.

When it was ready, Odysseus led
his men inside. "Now we will
trick the Trojans," he said.

"Hide the ships nearby," Odysseus told the Greeks. The armies pretended to sail away, leaving only the wooden horse behind.

The Trojans saw the Greeks sailing away. "We've won!" they cheered.

"Look, the Greeks have left us a gift," said the Trojans, looking at the wooden horse. They pushed it right up to the city gates.

Odysseus and his men kept very quiet. If they made a sound, their plan would fail.

But some of the Trojans were worried. "What if it's a trick?" asked one soldier. He threw his spear at the horse's belly.

Odysseus and his men kept very still. No one dared to move. "No, it's just a gift after all," the Trojans cried.

The Trojans opened the gates and pulled the huge horse into the city.

That night they had a great party to celebrate the end of the war.

When everyone was finally asleep,
Odysseus and his men leapt out.

They opened the city gates and all
the Greek soldiers charged into Troy.

The Trojans were shocked. They fought bravely but they could not stop Odysseus and the Greek army from destroying the whole of Troy.

29

Nothing was left of the city. People even forgot where it had stood.

But no one will ever forget the story of the great wooden horse.

Hopscotch has been specially designed to fit the requirements of the Literacy Framework. It offers real books by top authors and illustrators for children developing their reading skills. There are 63 Hopscotch stories to choose from:

Marvin, the Blue Pig
ISBN 978 0 7496 4619 6

Plip and Plop
ISBN 978 0 7496 4620 2

The Queen's Dragon
ISBN 978 0 7496 4618 9

Flora McQuack
ISBN 978 0 7496 4621 9

Willie the Whale
ISBN 978 0 7496 4623 3

Naughty Nancy
ISBN 978 0 7496 4622 6

Run!
ISBN 978 0 7496 4705 6

The Playground Snake
ISBN 978 0 7496 4706 3

"Sausages!"
ISBN 978 0 7496 4707 0

Bear in Town
ISBN 978 0 7496 5875 5

Pippin's Big Jump
ISBN 978 0 7496 4710 0

Whose Birthday Is It?
ISBN 978 0 7496 4709 4

The Princess and the Frog
ISBN 978 0 7496 5129 9

Flynn Flies High
ISBN 978 0 7496 5130 5

Clever Cat
ISBN 978 0 7496 5131 2

Moo!
ISBN 978 0 7496 5332 3

Izzie's Idea
ISBN 978 0 7496 5334 7

Roly-poly Rice Ball
ISBN 978 0 7496 5333 0

I Can't Stand It!
ISBN 978 0 7496 5765 9

Cockerel's Big Egg
ISBN 978 0 7496 5767 3

How to Teach a Dragon Manners
ISBN 978 0 7496 5873 1

The Truth about those Billy Goats
ISBN 978 0 7496 5766 6

Marlowe's Mum and the Tree House
ISBN 978 0 7496 5874 8

The Truth about Hansel and Gretel
ISBN 978 0 7496 4708 7

The Best Den Ever
ISBN 978 0 7496 5876 2

ADVENTURES

Aladdin and the Lamp
ISBN 978 0 7496 6692 7

Blackbeard the Pirate
ISBN 978 0 7496 6690 3

George and the Dragon
ISBN 978 0 7496 6691 0

Jack the Giant-Killer
ISBN 978 0 7496 6693 4

TALES OF KING ARTHUR

1. The Sword in the Stone
ISBN 978 0 7496 6694 1

2. Arthur the King
ISBN 978 0 7496 6695 8

3. The Round Table
ISBN 978 0 7496 6697 2

4. Sir Lancelot and the Ice Castle
ISBN 978 0 7496 6698 9

TALES OF ROBIN HOOD

Robin and the Knight
ISBN 978 0 7496 6699 6

Robin and the Monk
ISBN 978 0 7496 6700 9

Robin and the Silver Arrow
ISBN 978 0 7496 6703 0

Robin and the Friar
ISBN 978 0 7496 6702 3

FAIRY TALES

The Emperor's New Clothes
ISBN 978 0 7496 7421 2

Cinderella
ISBN 978 0 7496 7417 5

Snow White
ISBN 978 0 7496 7418 2

Jack and the Beanstalk
ISBN 978 0 7496 7422 9

The Three Billy Goats Gruff
ISBN 978 0 7496 7420 5

The Pied Piper of Hamelin
ISBN 978 0 7496 7419 9

Goldilocks and the Three Bears
ISBN 978 0 7496 7903 3

Hansel and Gretel
ISBN 978 0 7496 7904 0

The Three Little Pigs
ISBN 978 0 7496 7905 7

Rapunzel
ISBN 978 0 7496 7906 4

Little Red Riding Hood
ISBN 978 0 7496 7907 1

Rumpelstiltskin
ISBN 978 0 7496 7908 8

HISTORIES

Toby and the Great Fire of London
ISBN 978 0 7496 7410 6

Pocahontas the Peacemaker
ISBN 978 0 7496 7411 3

Grandma's Seaside Bloomers
ISBN 978 0 7496 7412 0

Hoorah for Mary Seacole
ISBN 978 0 7496 7413 7

Remember the 5th of November
ISBN 978 0 7496 7414 4

Tutankhamun and the Golden Chariot
ISBN 978 0 7496 7415 1

MYTHS

Icarus, the Boy Who Flew
ISBN 978 0 7496 7992 7 *
ISBN 978 0 7496 8000 8

Perseus and the Snake Monster
ISBN 978 0 7496 7993 4 *
ISBN 978 0 7496 8001 5

Odysseus and the Wooden Horse
ISBN 978 0 7496 7994 1 *
ISBN 978 0 7496 8002 2

Persephone and the Pomegranate Seeds
ISBN 978 0 7496 7995 8 *
ISBN 978 0 7496 8003 9

Romulus and Remus
ISBN 978 0 7496 7996 5 *
ISBN 978 0 7496 8004 6

Thor's Hammer
ISBN 978 0 7496 7997 2 *
ISBN 978 0 7496 8005 3

No Dinner for Anansi
ISBN 978 0 7496 7998 9 *
ISBN 978 0 7496 8006 0

Gelert the Brave
ISBN 978 0 7496 7999 6 *
ISBN 978 0 7496 8007 7

* hardback